Sheltie Leads the Way

Peter Clover

PUFFIN BOOKS

For Lesley Hadcroft

PUFFIN BOOKS

Published by the Penguin Group
Penguin Books Ltd, 27 Wrights Lane, London W8 5TZ, England
Penguin Putnam Inc., 375 Hudson Street, New York, New York 10014, USA
Penguin Books Australia Ltd, Ringwood, Victoria, Australia
Penguin Books Canada Ltd, 10 Alcorn Avenue, Toronto, Ontario, Canada M4V 3B2
Penguin Books (NZ) Ltd, 182–190 Wairau Road, Auckland 10, New Zealand

Penguin Books Ltd, Registered Offices: Harmondsworth, Middlesex, England

First published 1998
5

Created by Working Partners Ltd, London W12 7QY

Filmset in 14/20 Palatino

Made and printed in England by Clays Ltd, St Ives plc

British Library Cataloguing in Publication Data
A CIP catalogue record for this book is available from the British Library

ISBN 0-140-38952-0

PUFFIN BOOKS

Sheltie Leads the Way

Make friends with

The little pony with the big heart

Sheltie is the lovable little Shetland pony with a big personality. He is cheeky, full of fun and has a heart of gold. His best friend and new owner is Emma, and together they have lots of exciting adventures.

Share Sheltie and Emma's adventures in

SHELTIE THE SHETLAND PONY
SHELTIE SAVES THE DAY
SHELTIE AND THE RUNAWAY
SHELTIE FINDS A FRIEND
SHELTIE TO THE RESCUE
SHELTIE IN DANGER
SHELTIE RIDES TO WIN
SHELTIE AND THE SADDLE MYSTERY

Peter Clover was born and went to school in London. He was a storyboard artist and illustrator before he began to put words to his pictures. He enjoys painting, travelling, cooking and keeping fit, and lives on the coast in Somerset.

Also by Peter Clover in Puffin

The Sheltie Series

1: SHELTIE THE SHETLAND PONY
2: SHELTIE SAVES THE DAY
3: SHELTIE AND THE RUNAWAY
4: SHELTIE FINDS A FRIEND
5: SHELTIE TO THE RESCUE
6: SHELTIE IN DANGER
7: SHELTIE RIDES TO WIN
8: SHELTIE AND THE SADDLE MYSTERY
10: SHELTIE THE HERO
11: SHELTIE IN TROUBLE
12: SHELTIE AND THE STRAY
13: SHELTIE AND THE SNOW PONY
14: SHELTIE ON PARADE
15: SHELTIE FOR EVER
16: SHELTIE ON PATROL
17: SHELTIE GOES TO SCHOOL
18: SHELTIE GALLOPS AHEAD
19: SHELTIE IN DOUBLE TROUBLE
20: SHELTIE IN PERIL
21: SHELTIE BY THE SEA

Chapter One

Emma puffed out her chest and tried to look important.

'Stable management, it's called,' she said.

Mum and Dad looked at each other across the breakfast table and tried not to grin. Emma was taking this very seriously.

It was Tracy Diamond's birthday next Saturday. Tracy was one of

Emma's friends from school and she was getting a pony of her own.

Emma had bought Tracy a lovely book on caring for ponies, and although it was a birthday present for someone else, Emma had read it herself from cover to cover. Emma's favourite part was the chapter on stable management.

Emma knew all about mucking out and cleaning Sheltie's field shelter. She also knew how to keep the paddock clear and how to clean and polish Sheltie's tack. But what Emma didn't realize was that doing all these things made her a manager.

'If it's called stable management,' said Emma, 'then I'm a stable manager!'

Emma had copied a list from Tracy's birthday book into a little notepad. She had even drawn a picture of Sheltie, her little Shetland pony, on the front cover, with crayons.

Although Emma had been looking after Sheltie for quite a long time now, having a list to follow was a new game.

Emma liked being organized and Mum was really proud of her. Emma just wanted to do her very best for Sheltie.

After breakfast, her little brother, Joshua, followed Emma out to the tack room.

Emma read aloud to Joshua and checked off all the items on her special list one by one.

'Fork, trowel, shovel, stiff brush, wheelbarrow, bucket, strong gloves.'

Joshua listened, but he really didn't know what Emma was talking about.

'Sheltie's things,' said Joshua, pointing at the loaded wheelbarrow.

'Yes, that's right, Joshua,' said Emma. 'Sheltie's things. Now, help me push them into the paddock.'

Sheltie was in a very nosy mood and straight away he stuck his head into the wheelbarrow. First he found the bucket. Sheltie had already been fed his breakfast, but he knew that things to eat often came in buckets. This bucket was empty though. Sheltie whickered with disappointment. Then he found the gloves.

'Sheltie, leave those alone!' said Emma. But Sheltie had already snatched up one of the gloves with his teeth.

Emma tried to get the glove back. She should have known better. Sheltie loved this kind of game and

was soon dashing all round the paddock with Emma chasing him.

She finally caught up with Sheltie and took the glove away, but then Joshua picked up the second glove and threw it up in the air. Sheltie snatched it and galloped off again.

'Oh no, Joshua!' said Emma. And the chase was on once more.

Mum came down to the paddock to fetch Joshua. She was taking him with her to the Saturday market in the village, and smiled when she saw Emma chasing Sheltie.

Sheltie ran up to Mum and let her take the glove.

Emma came running up behind.

'I'm worn out already,' she said. 'And I haven't even started yet!'

Sheltie blew a soft snort and nuzzled Emma's arm.

'Dad's in the garage if you need him. See you later,' said Mum, and she left Emma to get on with her chores.

'Bye bye, Sheltie,' said Joshua.

Chapter Two

First, Emma cleaned the paddock with the trowel and bucket.

Then she went into the field shelter and began to rake out the old straw. Emma piled it all into the empty wheelbarrow. Later, Mr Crock would collect the bucket and the wheelbarrow. Mr Crock liked the manure for his roses, and he was using Sheltie's old bedding straw to fill a muddy ditch at the end of his garden.

Emma had been helping Mr Crock to spread the straw and stomp it into the mud. Sheltie had been helping too. He liked stomping on things.

Next, Emma swept the bare floor of the shelter and lay down some dry bedding. She filled Sheltie's hay net and topped up his water trough.

Sheltie watched all this with great interest. He knew that if he wasn't naughty and waited patiently, then Emma would give him a peppermint.

When Emma had finally finished, she flopped down on to the grass exhausted.

'There!' said Emma. 'I've done it.'

Sheltie whinnied, pushed his nose

down the back of Emma's collar and blew hot breath down her neck. It tickled and made Emma laugh. She gave Sheltie a peppermint as a treat and sat there as he crunched it in her ear.

That afternoon, the invitation to Tracy's birthday party arrived. It was addressed to Emma and Sheltie. Emma knew there was going to be a party, but she didn't realize that it was going to be a special pony party.

Listed on the invitation were the names of everyone else who had been invited. They all had ponies and their ponies were invited too!

There were eight names in all, including Tracy's and her own.

Emma already knew that Sally was going to the party because she had been there at school when Tracy had asked her.

Alice Parker's name was there too. Alice went to the same school as Emma and Sally, but she was in a different class.

Two boys from school were also going. Their names were Robert and Dylan.

Last on the list were two other girls who were friends of Tracy from the riding stables. Emma didn't know them, but their names were Charlotte and Joanna.

Emma felt really excited when she saw the invitation. She could hardly wait to read it aloud to Mum.

'There's even going to be a special scavenger hunt,' she said.

'Oh, that sounds fun, doesn't it?' said Mum.

Emma nodded. 'But what is a scavenger hunt?' she asked.

Mum smiled. 'It's a game, Emma.

Like a treasure hunt. Usually, everyone who's playing is given a list of things which they have to find. The person who gets the most things from the list is the winner.'

Emma's eyes grew wide with excitement. Lists were one of her favourite things at the moment. And searching for things on a list sounded brilliant.

Mum looked at the invitation.

'It seems the best bit, though, is that you'll get to do it all on your ponies,' said Mum. 'It says here at the bottom that it's a special "pony" scavenger hunt.'

'Wow! I didn't see that bit,' said Emma. Then she thought for a moment. 'So what sort of things will we have to look for?' she asked.

'A scavenger hunt can be for anything,' replied Mum. 'Anything at all. It depends on who is writing the list. When I was on a scavenger hunt once, two of the things we had to find were an ostrich feather and a swimming medal.'

'Where did you manage to find an ostrich?' asked Emma.

Mum laughed. 'Luckily, it was only a feather and not the whole bird we had to find. And grandma had a great big hat in her wardrobe covered with them.'

'Perhaps I should start collecting things now,' said Emma.

'That's not the idea,' Mum said, smiling. 'You're supposed to wait until you get the list. That's half the fun.'

Emma decided to telephone Sally straight away. She wanted to tell her best friend all about scavenger hunts. But first she went upstairs to her bedroom to fish out Dad's old swimming medals, just in case they were on the list.

Chapter Three

Next Saturday morning, the day of Tracy's birthday, Emma helped Mum make a special party cake for the ponies.

'This will be a nice surprise for Tracy,' said Emma as she chopped apples and carrots at the kitchen table.

Mum was busy stirring pony nuts with bran and hot water into a thick mushy mixture.

'Now, you stir in the apples and carrots, Emma,' said Mum. She pushed the bowl towards Emma and handed her a big wooden spoon.

Emma stirred everything together until it looked like thick, lumpy porridge. Then she watched Mum pour it into a round cake tin and press the top down with a plate.

When it had cooled, Mum said, 'Now let's turn it out.'

They turned the whole thing upside down and when Mum lifted the tin off they had a nice pony cake sitting on the plate.

'That's fantastic,' said Emma. 'It looks almost good enough for me to eat.'

Mum sprinkled some loose oats on

top and laughed. 'I think it looks better to you than it might taste. But I know who will like it.'

Emma grinned. 'I'd better hide it from Sheltie until we get to the party,' she said.

Mum put the pony cake into a cardboard box and tied it with string. 'There! It's ready when you are.'

Emma went upstairs to change and came down in her riding gear, with her present for Tracy wrapped in bright paper and ribbon.

Mum put the pony cake into a plastic carrier bag with Tracy's present on top.

'Will you be able to ride and carry this lot, Emma?' she asked.

'Of course,' said Emma. 'Sheltie's brilliant. I can ride him with it propped in front of me on the saddle.'

Sheltie was in the paddock already tacked up and ready to go. When he saw Emma he opened his big brown eyes wide. He knew what was coming. It was time for a ride.

Emma pushed Sheltie's forelock out of his eyes before she mounted, then set off down the lane to meet Sally and Minnow. The two girls and their ponies were going to ride over to Tracy's together.

Tracy lived on the far side of Little Applewood, behind Barrow Hill. Emma and Sheltie had often been riding there. They both knew all the surrounding countryside really well.

'I've only been riding out this way once before,' said Sally. Normally she rode with Emma and Sheltie on the other side of Little Applewood, near

Horseshoe Pond and the hills beyond.

'Sheltie seems to know his way around,' she continued. She leaned forward and gave Minnow a reassuring pat. Minnow was looking at the unfamiliar countryside and

whinnied softly. But he was happy to walk along next to Sheltie.

Sheltie took a deep breath and sniffed the air. He could smell the pony cake even though it was in a box and a plastic bag. Sheltie snorted and licked his lips.

'Do you know what kind of pony Tracy is getting?' asked Sally.

'It's Blaze, the strawberry roan from the riding stables,' said Emma. 'Tracy has been having riding lessons for months and she always rides Blaze. Now her mum and dad are buying Blaze from the owners so Tracy will have her all to herself.'

'That's great,' said Sally. 'I like Tracy. Perhaps she'll be able to come out riding with us now that she's got her own pony.'

Just then, the lane they were riding along opened out to fields on either side. The hedges had been cut back and were low enough for Emma and Sally to see over.

Sheltie let out a sigh of contentment and stopped to snatch lazily at a piece of greenery. Suddenly he jumped back in surprise as a large bull poked its head over the hedge and let out a loud bellow.

Minnow was startled too and lurched sideways. He almost bumped into Sheltie.

The bull stood looking at the two ponies.

'Wow!' said Emma. 'That made Sheltie jump!'

'It made Minnow jump too,' said Sally. 'We weren't expecting that, were we, boy?' She gave Minnow a pat to settle him down.

'I didn't know Marjorie and Todd kept a bull in their field,' said Emma.

'Maybe they've just let the field to a farmer,' said Sally. 'Or perhaps they're looking after it. Marjorie and Todd keep all kinds of animals, don't they?'

The two girls sat for a while, staring at the bull. The bull stared back. Then Sheltie blew a raspberry and jangled his bit restlessly.

'I wouldn't want to mess with him if I were you, Sheltie,' said Sally. 'He's enormous.'

But Sheltie wasn't scared. Once he had got over the shock of the bull's sudden appearance, Sheltie edged closer for a better look.

The bull bellowed again. Sheltie's ears flattened against his head and he looked rather nervous.

'Come on, Sheltie,' said Emma. 'Let's leave him alone.' Then she squeezed with her legs and they walked on.

Chapter Four

Tracy lived further up the lane, about ten minutes' ride away in a white stonewashed house called Redroofs.

Emma could see the red roof-tiles above the trees ahead, in a hollow behind Barrow Hill.

When Emma and Sally finally ambled up the drive to the house, they could see other ponies already in the back paddock.

Emma recognized Alice Parker on Blue and Robert and Dylan with their two ponies, Toffee and Sabre. Then she saw Tracy sitting up on Blaze and gave a friendly wave.

Tracy waved back and trotted over to the paddock gate to greet them.

Emma could see that a long table had been set up in the paddock. It was laid with a white cloth, plates and mugs. There was a huge platter of sandwiches at one end, with fruit jellies and a birthday cake at the other.

'Hello, you two,' said Tracy happily. 'Say hello to Blaze. Isn't she wonderful?'

Emma and Sally agreed. Blaze was such a pretty pony. She was not much bigger than Sheltie and was a similar light-chestnut colour, flecked with white. She had a beautiful, thick tail and mane and a white blaze.

Straight away Sheltie made friends with the little pony. He pushed his nose towards Blaze and sniffed her muzzle. Then he made a low whicker in his throat and swished his long tail.

'I think Sheltie likes Blaze,' said Tracy. 'She is beautiful, isn't she, Sheltie?'

Minnow said hello too, and rubbed noses with Blaze across the top of the gate. Tracy let Emma and Sally into the paddock as Robert and Dylan came over on foot. They had already turned their ponies out to graze.

Sheltie sniffed and poked at Dylan's jacket pocket, looking for a treat.

'Behave yourself, Sheltie,' laughed Emma. 'Don't be so rude.'

'It's all right,' Dylan said with a

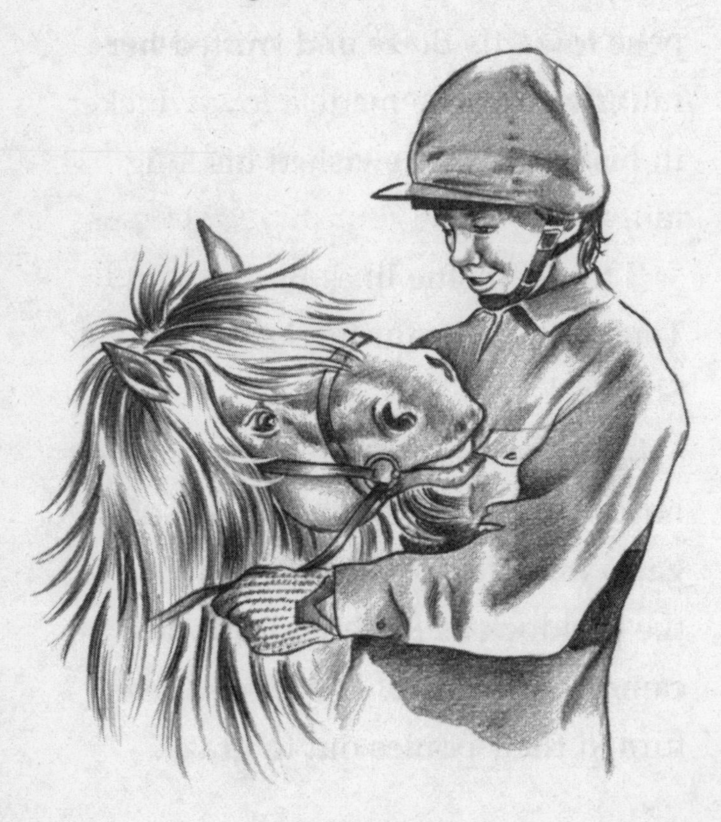

grin. 'He must know I always carry peppermints for Sabre.'

'Sheltie can smell a mint a mile off,' said Emma. 'He's got a nose for them.'

Dylan palmed both Sheltie and Minnow a treat and the two ponies crunched their mints happily.

The other two girls arrived on almost identical ponies. Both ponies were black, and the only way to tell them apart was that one pony had a white sock.

Charlotte and Joanna were also twins. They were almost identical too. Luckily they both wore little silver necklaces with their initials hanging from them, which helped Emma to tell them apart.

Sheltie snorted a friendly welcome to Jet and Inky, the twins' ponies.

Everyone seemed to like Sheltie straight away. He was so cheeky and enjoyed all the attention he was getting. Being a little Shetland, he was different from all the other

ponies. He was the smallest of the ponies, but Emma thought he had the biggest personality of them all.

When everyone had turned out their ponies to frolic and play together in the paddock, it was Sheltie who seemed to be leading all the games. Sheltie chased the other ponies here and there. Then he rounded them up in a corner before dashing off again with them all racing after him.

Emma and Sally gave Tracy her birthday presents. Then Emma handed the pony cake over to Tracy's mum.

'What a lovely idea,' said Mrs Diamond. She set the pony treat down on the table next to Tracy's own birthday cake. It looked splendid.

'I've never seen a pony cake before,' said the twins together. And neither had anyone else.

Sheltie came galloping over with all the other ponies hot on his heels.

'I know someone who'd like a big slice of that,' said Emma as they settled around the table.

'I'll give all the ponies a piece when we cut Tracy's cake,' said Mrs Diamond. But Sheltie couldn't wait that long. The table was level with Sheltie's nose and he reached forward to help himself.

'Sheltie!' Emma warned sternly.

Sheltie stopped immediately and looked at Emma through his long

forelock. Sheltie's big brown eyes sparkled, but he did as he was told. He stood there and waited while the party guests tucked into the sandwiches and jellies.

Next, Tracy opened her birthday presents. Sally had given her a model pony to make. The twins gave her a

T-shirt with 'Pony Crazy' embroidered across the front. Dylan's present was a plastic lunch box with a pony on the lid that looked just like Blaze. Robert had bought a pony jigsaw puzzle and Alice gave Tracy a multicoloured headband.

Tracy loved all her presents, particularly Emma's pony book.

'I'll teach you all about stable management if you like,' offered Emma.

'She's an expert,' winked Sally. Then she poked Emma in the ribs.

Chapter Five

When it was time to cut the cakes, Sheltie did his funny stomping dance. He was very excited.

Sheltie was given the first piece as he had been waiting so patiently. He gobbled the cake down in seconds.

Blaze was more delicate and nibbled daintily at her slice.

Sheltie hung around hoping for

another piece. But when he realized there was no more, he snatched a spare sandwich and ran off with it across the paddock.

'I bet you have a lot of fun with Sheltie, Emma!' laughed Tracy.

'He may be small,' said Emma, 'but he's a giant handful at times.'

Sheltie blew a loud raspberry from across the paddock.

Mr Diamond joined the party when they had finished the food. He had been busy preparing the lists for the scavenger hunt. As Mrs Diamond cleared away the table her husband handed out felt-tipped pens and clipboards with a sheet of paper attached to each.

This was the part Emma had been

waiting for. The special 'pony' scavenger hunt.

'Right,' said Mr Diamond. 'Here are your lists. There are ten things you have to find. And the first and last are in riddles. You have two hours to search for everything and you must be back here by four o'clock prompt.'

Emma quickly looked at the items on the paper and read the list out loud to Sally. 'The first one's a riddle:

'You can't go riding without them
And they're always on the floor.
There's even a pond named after ONE,
But you must bring home FOUR.'

'That's easy,' she said smiling.

'What is it then?' asked Sally. She looked puzzled.

'Horseshoes,' whispered Emma so the others wouldn't hear. 'And everyone's already got them,' she added.

'So it's a trick,' said Sally. 'That's clever. What else is on the list?'

Emma continued: 'A pine cone, a black feather, a length of rope, a conker, a thistle, a wild mushroom, a piece of heather, some sheep's wool and the second riddle – a hero's autograph.'

Emma was disappointed to find that there was no swimming medal on the list. But she was thrilled to see that a length of rope was one of the things they had to find. Emma always carried a rope with her, clipped to one of Sheltie's saddle rings, like a cowgirl.

'I told you rope always comes in handy,' said Emma. It was her turn to poke Sally in the ribs now.

The party was already teamed up in twos for safety and to make things easier. The twins couldn't be separated, because their ponies Jet and Inky always went everywhere together, so they were the first pair. Emma was with Sally. Tracy, being a

beginner, teamed up with Alice, who was an experienced rider. The two boys were happy to be together.

'Boy power!' they said. 'It's the boys against the girls.'

Everyone laughed and they were all keen to get going.

'Come on, Sally,' said Emma. 'There's a chestnut tree for the conker at Horseshoe Pond. We can start there and work our way back. Let's go!'

'We'll give them boy power,' Sally said, smiling. 'Wait till we show them girl power!'

They squeezed with their legs and urged Sheltie and Minnow into a trot.

It was a warm autumn afternoon,

but the sky was beginning to turn a little hazy.

On the way to Horseshoe Pond they found a pine cone and a feather. The feather wasn't a black one, but Emma soon made it black with the felt tip.

'There!' she said. 'One black feather.'

'Isn't that cheating?' said Sally.

'Of course not,' grinned Emma cheekily. 'That's four things already. Horseshoes, pine cone, rope and a feather! We must be in the lead.'

At Horseshoe Pond they found their conker. They took a good look around, but couldn't see any sign of the other teams.

'I wonder where they all are,' said Sally.

'They're not as clever as us, are

they, Sheltie?' laughed Emma. She clapped his rump.

Sheltie shook out his mane and bent down to nibble on a thistle.

'Well done, Sheltie,' said Emma, pulling up his head. 'You've found a thistle. Clever boy. But don't eat it!'

'That's six things now, leaving only four to go,' said Sally. She read from the clipboard: 'A wild mushroom, heather, sheep's wool, and the riddle – a hero's autograph.'

'We'll find heather and sheep's wool on the moor,' said Emma confidently. 'And there might be wild mushrooms in the fields on the way.'

'What about the hero's autograph?' said Sally. 'I can't work that one out! How many heroes do you know?'

'We'll have to think about that last,' said Emma. 'It's trickier than the first riddle.'

'Come on, then,' said Sally, glancing at her watch. 'We've just over an hour left. Let's head for the moor and look for mushrooms on the way.'

As they rode Sheltie and Minnow along the bridle path through the woods, they met Tracy and Alice. Tracy waved the black feather she was holding, but didn't stop to chat. They just exchanged smiles and urged their ponies into a canter. Time was precious.

Later they saw Dylan and Robert flying along on a lower path. Sheltie heard them first and let out a long whinny. The two boys were whooping and laughing as they rode by. There was no sign of the twins though!

Chapter Six

Emma and Sally made their way to the flat fields at the foot of Barrow Hill. They slipped out of their saddles and led Sheltie and Minnow through the gate to look for wild mushrooms.

'I hope this isn't the bull's field,' said Sally.

'I don't think so,' answered Emma. 'That field was further over there.' She waved her arm and pointed across to their right. But they had come back a different way, and Emma wasn't really quite certain.

Sheltie was into everything. He poked his nose among the long grass and sniffed in the hedge and at the drifts of fallen leaves.

'Come on, Sheltie,' said Emma. 'Find us some nice juicy mushrooms.'

'But don't let him eat any,' said Sally. 'They might be poisonous!'

Emma gave Sheltie a loose rein and kept a keen eye on everything he was interested in.

Sheltie sniffled and snorted, then suddenly he stopped. A clump of bushy ferns was growing near the hedge. Sheltie pawed the ground with his hoof and neighed softly. Then he blew through his lips and pushed his nose into the ferns. Sheltie sneezed.

Emma parted the ferns with her toe, and there, nestling among the green fronds, was a clump of wild field-mushrooms.

'Mushrooms always make Sheltie sneeze,' said Emma. Sheltie jangled his reins and sneezed again as Emma knelt to pick one.

'Now for the sheep's wool and heather,' said Emma, getting back into the saddle.

They were riding Sheltie and Minnow side by side across the field when suddenly Sally said, 'Emma, have you noticed anything?'

'Such as?' Emma asked.

'Listen,' said Sally. 'Keep Sheltie moving, but listen hard.'

Sheltie's ears had already twitched backwards. He had heard something long before Sally. Emma strained her ears. And sure enough, soft but heavy animal footsteps were falling behind them.

Emma turned her head slowly, but kept Sheltie walking. Then she gasped when she saw what was coming. Lumbering up after them was the bull. They were in the same field after all.

'Quick,' urged Emma. 'Gallop to the gate!'

Both ponies raced across the field. Emma opened the gate as quickly as possible and they bustled Sheltie and Minnow through. Sally managed to close the gate just seconds before the bull pushed its huge head over the rails and bellowed loudly.

'Phew!' gasped Sally. 'That was a close one.'

Emma grinned sheepishly. They had just had a very narrow escape.

Chapter Seven

As they carried on to the top of Barrow Hill the air suddenly turned cool and damp. Both girls noticed, as they rode over the crest, that the sky was now hazy and a white mist was sitting low across the moor.

'We'd better not go in too far,' said Sally. 'It looks really foggy over there.'

'We'll only go as far as Saxon's

Cross,' said Emma. 'There are always sheep over there. Once we've found the wool and heather, we've got everything except the hero's autograph. I still can't work that one out! It must be something we can find easily in Little Applewood. But how many heroes are there living here?'

'I've got it!' exclaimed Sally. 'It must be Mr Samson's sweetshop. His paper bags have his signature written across them, don't they? That's the riddle. Samson was a hero, wasn't he? So it's a paper bag with Samson written on it. A hero's autograph!'

'You're brilliant, Sally,' said Emma. 'On the way back we can buy some sweets and get a bag. I bet nobody else will ever work that one out. A hero's autograph. Fantastic.'

As they rode across the moor to Saxon's Cross, Emma and Sally kept a lookout for heather and any stray tufts of sheep's wool clinging to the gorse. But they didn't have much luck. They rode further on to the moor and the mist thickened.

'There!' yelled Emma. She leaped out of the saddle and picked up a nice cloud of wool from a bush. Sheltie gave it a sniff as Emma held it up for Sally to see.

Then Emma noticed that some heather was also growing near by.

'We've done it! We've got

everything,' said Emma.

'Except the sweet bag,' Sally reminded her. 'But that's easy now, isn't it?'

They had stuffed all their treasures into various pockets and were ready to ride back into the village when

Sheltie suddenly pricked up his ears and blew a really loud snort. He lifted his head high and looked out across the moor.

Sheltie had heard something. His sharp ears had picked up a distant cry for help.

Minnow had heard something too!

'What is it, boy?' said Emma. She followed Sheltie's stare. Then she heard a voice calling and saw a rider on a black pony coming towards them through a thick curtain of mist.

'Is that one of the twins?' said Emma.

'Come on,' said Sally. 'Someone's in trouble.'

The girls squeezed Sheltie and Minnow into a gallop and quickly covered the short distance. The white fog swirled around the ponies' legs. It was almost as though they were riding across a cloud. And by the time they reached the black pony they were staring blindly into a white wall of fog. They could just about see the rider in front of them.

'Is that you, Joanna?' said Emma.

'No, it's me . . . Charlotte. Something terrible has happened. Inky is stuck in a bog. We were riding the moor looking for sheep's wool and the mist came. It happened so quickly we didn't have a chance. Then we stumbled across the bog and now Inky's stuck. It's not very deep, but he's so frightened. I didn't want to leave them, but I had to try and get help.' Charlotte paused for breath. She looked so worried.

Emma quickly looked around. Behind her she could see two other riders faintly silhouetted against the rise of the hill. It was Robert and Dylan.

'Sally, you ride back and tell them what's happened,' said Emma. 'I'll go with Charlotte to find Joanna and Inky. Tell the boys to follow on, but if you see Tracy and Alice, get them to go and fetch help. The nearest house is Marjorie and Todd's cottage at the foot of the hill. You stay on top of the Barrow, Sally, and watch where we go. We're going to need someone up there to keep watch and point the way.'

'Do be careful, Emma,' said Sally. Then she turned Minnow and galloped away.

Chapter Eight

The two boys saw Sally coming out of the mist and rode down to meet her halfway. Emma was watching, and as she glanced up to the Barrow she spotted Tracy and Alice appear on the rise.

Good, she thought. Sally will get them to go for help.

Robert and Dylan galloped on to the moor as Emma and Charlotte disappeared slowly into the mist.

'We'll take it nice and steady, Sheltie,' Emma said, 'so the boys can follow us.' Then she slipped out of the saddle and snapped a twig from a gorse bush.

'I'll leave a marker as well, so we can find our way back,' said Emma. She used paper from the clipboard to make a flag and pushed the twig into the soft grass.

As Emma climbed back into the saddle, Robert and Dylan rode up.

'Perhaps if we call out, Joanna will hear us,' said Robert. 'She can't be far away.'

'No, she's not far,' said Charlotte. 'We just can't see her!'

They began calling. Then they

stopped to listen. They couldn't hear anything, but Sheltie could. His ears twitched, then stood to attention. He raised his nose and sniffed at the damp air.

Sheltie caught Inky's scent straight away and blew a series of loud

snorts, then pawed the ground excitedly.

'Sheltie knows where they are,' said Emma. 'I'm certain of it.' She loosened the reins and let Sheltie lead the way.

The group of riders stayed close together and continued calling to Joanna. Sheltie joined in with a series of neighs and loud whinnies, which echoed across the moor.

Then suddenly, through the fog came an answering call from another pony.

'I can hear something!' said Emma. They all listened carefully.

'Yes, so can I,' said Charlotte.

It was Joanna calling. 'Over here! Over here!'

They could all hear it quite clearly.

'She's not far now,' said Charlotte. 'We're coming, Jo!' she yelled.

'Keep calling,' urged Emma, 'so we can follow your voice!'

Suddenly the ground became wet and soggy. Small patches of bog were all around them. And they could see Joanna and Inky up ahead, as dark shadows in the mist.

They trod very carefully, the ponies picking their way through the muddy patches. When they reached Joanna she burst into tears.

Poor Inky was standing up to his fetlocks in a sticky bog, and couldn't move.

The first thing Emma did was give Joanna a hug. 'It's all right, we're here to try and help,' Emma reassured her. Sheltie rubbed noses with Inky and blew softly.

Robert and Dylan spoke gently to Inky and tried to calm the frightened pony.

All four of Inky's hoofs were well and truly stuck. Dylan reached

forward and caught hold of Inky's bridle reins. He tried to encourage the pony to make an extra effort and step out of the bog. But it was impossible. Inky was too frightened, and wouldn't even lift one hoof.

Then Emma had an idea. She suddenly remembered how Mr Crock was using Sheltie's old straw to fill his muddy ditch.

'We need to put something down in front of him,' she said. 'Something to mash into the mud. Something to lay across the bog and make it more solid.'

'What about some bracken and heather?' said Robert.

Charlotte held the other ponies a safe distance away while they set to

work gathering the clumps of bracken and heather which they spread out in front of Inky.

Sheltie helped by treading the blanket of undergrowth into the mud. He had done it before in Mr Crock's ditch, and he copied what Emma was doing. Each time fresh bracken was laid down, Sheltie trampled it into the bog.

Soon they had made a surface which was firm enough for them to stand on without sinking too much themselves. Emma held Sheltie while he stretched his neck forward to touch noses with Inky again and whickered softly. Inky seemed really pleased that Sheltie was there.

'Right,' said Emma. 'Let's try and lift one of his feet out on to the bedding.'

Chapter Nine

Robert and Dylan stood on either side of Inky. Joanna stood at his head and stroked the pony's muzzle as the boys made a tremendous effort to lift a front leg. With a wet, slurping, squelching sound, they managed to lift it free.

With one leg on firmer ground, Inky was able to use his own strength and pull his other front hoof free almost on his own. But with his extra weight on the makeshift matting, he slowly began to sink.

'Oh no!' sobbed Joanna. 'What's happening?'

'We need more bedding, and quickly!' yelled Emma.

They hurriedly gathered more bracken and heather. Their hands were getting scratched to pieces, but they had to carry on and try to free Inky. They carried heaps of heather and ferns and laid a whole new bed beneath the frightened pony.

Again, Sheltie helped by treading everything down and Inky was now able to lift his own front legs and stand half out of the bog.

Inky's hind legs were a bit trickier

though, as they were carrying most of his weight.

'Can't we just pull him?' suggested Robert.

'No, that won't do it,' said Emma. 'I've got a better idea.' She called everyone over.

'If Robert and I link hands and stand on either side of Inky, we can push him from behind with our arms,' said Emma. 'It might be enough to help him out of the bog on his own.'

Inky stood very still. He seemed to know that everyone was trying to help him, but he was still very frightened.

Sheltie stood in front of Inky with Joanna and made soft pony noises, while Emma and Robert stood in place at the back.

'Right. Let's give it a try!' said Emma. *'Push!'*

Joanna pulled on his bridle at the

same time, and Inky struggled to move forward. But the boggy mud was like thick tar around Inky's rear hoofs.

'Keep pushing, Robert,' yelled Emma.

Inky tried to lift his hind legs. Joanna and Sheltie urged him to try harder. But it was no good. His legs were stuck fast. And the pony was too frightened and tired to try any more.

'It's no use. We need more help,' said Emma. 'And this fog is getting thicker by the minute.'

It was true. No one had noticed just how thick the mist had become.

'Alice and Tracy must have got help by now,' said Emma. 'Where are they?'

'Perhaps one of us should ride out and let them know where we are,' said Robert. 'Maybe they can't find us!'

'But which way is it?' said Dylan as he looked around. 'It's so thick, we can't see a thing. Which way should we go?'

It was true. With the white mist surrounding them, they had totally lost their bearings.

Emma looked around. She didn't know which way either. Then she had an idea. She reached for Sheltie and whispered in his ear.

'You know, don't you, boy! Which way is it? Can you lead me out of here?'

Sheltie nodded his head and

pawed at the grass with his hoof. Then he flared his nostrils wide and sniffed at the foggy air.

In a flash, Emma was up in the saddle. She slackened the reins to make it easier for Sheltie to lead the way.

'Don't move from here,' called Emma over her shoulder. 'Keep Inky calm.' Then she and Sheltie were gone into the mist.

Chapter Ten

Sheltie trod slowly and carefully, avoiding any boggy patches. It seemed as though they had been walking for ages and the wall of fog remained thick and white. For a moment, Emma wondered if Sheltie really knew where he was going. But Sheltie was such a clever pony that she knew he could find his way anywhere.

Just then, Emma saw her marker flag.

'Good boy, Sheltie,' said Emma. She clapped Sheltie's neck and urged him to walk faster. They were definitely heading the right way.

The fog thinned out a little, and up ahead Emma thought she heard voices. Sheltie's ears pricked up. He could hear voices too, but he was more interested in the sound of heavy footfalls directly in front of him. Something very big was heading towards them.

Sheltie took a big sniff and gave a worried snort. The heavy sound was definitely not a pony, or a person. It was something much bigger.

Suddenly Sheltie stopped in his

tracks as the huge shape of a bull appeared before them. Emma gasped in horror. Oh no!

She felt her stomach somersault and her heart bang against her ribs. It was the bull they had been chased by earlier, in Marjorie's field. And now it was right in front of them!

Then Emma saw that the bull was wearing a leather harness, and the strong rope attached to it was being held by a figure. Two more steps and old Todd came into view, with the mist swirling at his feet. Marjorie was behind him. The bull was leading them like a big pet dog.

'Emma, is that you?' Marjorie's voice was unmistakable. 'Thank goodness we've found you.'

The picture of Marjorie and Todd with the huge bull was such a strange sight that Emma found herself grinning. Sheltie took a deep breath and let out a long snort of relief.

'This is Bruno,' said Marjorie. 'He's

the latest member of our family, and he's come to help.'

Emma was so relieved. For a moment she thought they were in terrible danger. But Bruno turned out to be as gentle as a lamb.

Emma quickly told Marjorie and Todd what had happened and Sheltie led the rescue party back through the fog to find Inky. The poor pony still had his back legs well and truly stuck.

Bruno was very big and very strong. Todd crossed two lunge ropes behind Inky's rump and fixed them in front to the bull's harness. As Bruno pulled, the lunge ropes lifted and pushed Inky from behind. At the first attempt, Bruno pulled Inky clear of the bog. The muddy goo around the pony's hind legs squelched and popped as he came clear and walked free to stand at last on solid ground.

'Thank goodness you're all safe and sound!' exclaimed Marjorie. 'The moor can be treacherous when a thick mist like this settles in. If it

wasn't for Sheltie, we would never have found you.'

Emma beamed her biggest smile. 'Good old Sheltie.'

'Do you think Sheltie can lead us out again?' said Marjorie.

Emma rubbed Sheltie's mane. 'Of course he can. Can't you, boy?'

Sheltie raised his head and neighed. His feet were dancing excitedly.

'A nice steady ride back,' Marjorie said. 'I think everyone has had enough excitement for one day, Sheltie.'

Chapter Eleven

They met up with Sally, Tracy and Alice up on the Barrow. And back at Redroofs Emma retold the story of the moorland rescue.

The sky was bright and clear once again and it was hard to imagine that there had been thick fog and danger out on the moor.

'You should have seen them when they came out of the mist,' said Tracy.

'It was fantastic. First we saw Sheltie. Then we saw big Bruno and all the other ponies behind.'

'Well, I think you were all very brave,' said Mrs Diamond. 'And very clever to think up such a brilliant idea to pad out the bog like that.'

'It was Emma who thought that one up,' said Robert.

Emma's face blushed a bright red.

'And don't forget Sheltie,' she said. 'He was the one who led us all to safety.'

'How could anyone forget Sheltie?' said Mrs Diamond. 'He's a real hero.'

With that, Sally jumped up and grabbed a piece of paper from the table. She lay it on the grass in front of Sheltie. Everyone looked puzzled as Sally coaxed Sheltie to mark the paper with a hoofprint.

'What's she up to?' said Tracy.

'There!' exclaimed Sally. 'A hero's autograph. The last item on the list. We've got everything now, Emma.'

With all the excitement, the others had completely forgotten about the scavenger hunt.

'Yes, Sally. You're right,' said Emma. 'Does anyone else have everything on the list?'

She looked around laughing. No one else did, so Emma and Sally had won.

'Trust you two,' Alice Parker said, smiling. 'But then you did have the advantage of having Sheltie on your team. How could you ever lose?'

'Pony power,' said Emma, and she exchanged a huge grin with Sally.

Not wanting to be left out, Sheltie

blew a hero's raspberry, and made everyone roar with laughter.